Charlie Baillie
Chairman and Chief Executive Officer
TD Bank Financial Group

Dear readers,

This book is for you!

It's a gift from TD to take home and treasure. I hope you enjoy books as much as I do. I especially hope you enjoy this book, *Nicholas at the Library*. It's the story of a boy who finds that the library is a great place to uncover amazing adventures inside books.

Everyone at TD is excited to give you and every grade 1 student in Canada this book. It's our way of celebrating TD Canadian Children's Book Week. It's also our way of inviting you to visit your local library, discover the magic world of books, and the fun of reading!

Have fun reading…just like Nicholas!

Charlie Baillie

Charlie Baillie

TD Bank Financial Group

Hazel Hutchins   Ruth Ohi

Nicholas at the Library

Annick Press

TD Canadian Children's Book Week

TD Bank Financial Group and the Canadian Children's Book Centre (CCBC) are pleased to present this book in celebration of TD Canadian Children's Book Week, Canada's largest annual festival of reading and Canadian children's literature.

Each November, Canadian authors, illustrators and storytellers tour from coast to coast to meet tens of thousands of young readers and share the special joy of books created for and about Canadian children. For more information about Canada's largest literary event for children, including readings, book signings and other festivities in your area, visit the CCBC's Book Week web site at www.bookweek.net.

The Canadian Children's Book Centre is a national, non-profit organization founded in 1976 to encourage reading, inspire fine children's book writing and illustration, promote Canadian children's literature and help the Canadian children's book industry grow.

TD Canadian Children's Book Week is made possible through the generous support of the following sponsors and funders: Title Sponsor, TD Bank Financial Group; Major Funder, The Canada Council for the Arts; Co-Associate Sponsors, Imperial Oil Charitable Foundation and Pearson Education Canada.

Special thanks to Annick Press for making this book available.

Second printing, November, 1991
Revised edition - May 1999, September 2000

Annick Press Ltd.

Annick Press gratefully acknowledges the support of The Canada Council for the Arts and the Ontario Arts Council.

Canadian Cataloguing in Publication Data

Hutchins, H.J. (Hazel J.)
Nicholas at the library

ISBN 1-55037-134-7 (bound).   ISBN 1-55037-132-0 (pbk.)

I. Ohi, Ruth. II. Title.

PS8565.U72N52 1990   jC813',54   C90-094523-0
PZ7. H87Ni 1990

Distribution for Canada and the USA:

Firefly Book Ltd.
3680 Victoria Park Avenue,
Willowdale, Ontario M2H 3K1

Printed in Canada by Friesens Corporation

The day it was raining Nicholas's mother said, "I know what we'll do – we'll go to the library."

Nicholas did not want to go to the library. Nicholas wanted to have twenty-three friends over to his house so they could run and shout and build forts and jump off the furniture and play wildly up and down the halls.

But his mother found the book bag and Nicholas had to go to the library.

The library was very quiet and very full of books. Nicholas decided to build a fort.

He took six books from the A section. He took nine books from the J section. He took twelve books from the O section and stopped.

There was a chimpanzee hiding in the O section – just a small chimpanzee, the kind that could ride in a pencil case or bathe in a cereal bowl. And it would not come out.

Nicholas went to his mother. "There's a chimpanzee in the O section," he said, "just a small chimpanzee – the kind that could ride in a pencil case or bathe in a cereal bowl. And it won't come out."

"You have a wonderful imagination and I love you very much," said his mother.

Nicholas checked the chimpanzee. It didn't look like imagination to him.

Nicholas went to the man behind the desk. "There is a chimpanzee in the O section," said Nicholas, "just a small chimpanzee – the kind that could ride in a pencil case or bathe in a cereal bowl. And it won't come out."

"Does it have a book card?" asked the man. "I can't deal with anything that doesn't have a card."

Nicholas went back to the chimpanzee. It didn't have a card. And it still wouldn't come out.

Nicholas peered around the corner of the head librarian's office. There were stacks of important papers and tubs of important pens and three important telephones.

"Hello, Nicholas," said the head librarian. "Have you been building book-forts again?"

"There is a chimpanzee in the O section," said Nicholas, "just a small chimpanzee – the kind that could ride in a pencil case or bathe in a cereal bowl. And it won't come out."

Together they went to the O section. There was the chimpanzee.

"Dear me," said the head librarian.

"If it won't come out, how can I play with it?" asked Nicholas.

"It's not a playing chimpanzee," said the head librarian. "It's a lost-story chimpanzee. If it doesn't find its way back soon, it's going to be a gone-forever chimpanzee."

"Gone forever?" asked Nicholas.

The chimpanzee gave a small, plaintive moan. One arm reached upward in a grasping motion.

"Isn't there something we can do?" asked Nicholas.

She consulted her Head Librarians' Manual.

"The only hope for a lost story is rapid search and rescue with the librarian's emergency ring." She pressed a strip of cardboard from the page, turned it (in a loop) and fastened the tab. "Except I don't think it's large enough for me."

"I could wear it," said Nicholas.

The head librarian looked at him sideways.

"I could," said Nicholas firmly.

The chimpanzee scrambled onto the cuff of his jeans. The head librarian took his hand.

"Stand on the nearest book," she said. "Think of places where chimpanzees might be, and put on the ring."

The library vanished. A smooth, melting feeling swept over Nicholas – then suddenly he couldn't breathe!

"Swim, Nicholas!"

Nicholas burst to the water's surface with the chimpanzee bobbing large as life beside him. A wave swept them onto a beach of warm, soft sand.

"Where are we?" asked Nicholas in amazement.

"It feels like a classic," said the head librarian. *"Robinson Crusoe, Swiss Family Robinson . . ."*

"You mean we're inside a book?" asked Nicholas.

"An exciting one," she said, "with wild animals and head-hunters and –"

"Head-hunters!" said Nicholas. The chimpanzee gave a howl and leapt into his arms. "I don't think this is the right place," said Nicholas.

"It will only take a moment to run through it," said the head librarian. "And remember, when we get to the back cover – jump!"

They began to run. They ran into the book, slowly at first. Then faster and faster they raced, past wild animals and quicksand and jungle fires. They brushed against terror and sadness and relief and adventure.

Nicholas saw a great volcano rising out of the story. "Wait!" he called. He'd always wanted to know about volcanoes.

"No time," cried the head librarian. "You can come back later, when you can read. Jump!"

They jumped into coldness. They jumped into snow!

"This would be a strange place for a chimpanzee," said the head librarian.

The chimpanzee zipped gaily past on a pair of skis.

"And my mother thinks I have an imagination," said Nicholas.

It was a short book. Already Nicholas could feel the back cover approaching.

"Jump!" he cried.

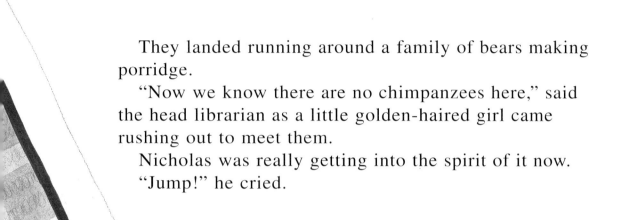

They landed running around a family of bears making porridge.

"Now we know there are no chimpanzees here," said the head librarian as a little golden-haired girl came rushing out to meet them.

Nicholas was really getting into the spirit of it now. "Jump!" he cried.

They galloped through farm books. They raced through Christmas books. They climbed mountains, drove trucks and rode on covered wagons. They sailed through ocean books. They traversed whole alphabets and went to bed one hundred and twenty-seven times.

Some books felt scary the moment Nicholas jumped into them, and others were like a hot summer day, or a song, or the smell of pepper.

But there was no place for a lost chimpanzee.

"Maybe here!" called Nicholas as they jumped into a circus parade, but all the animals were already in place.

"Surely this is it!" cried the head librarian as they raced through a zoo book.

All the cages were already full.

"Jump!" cried Nicholas.

In the last book, on the last page, they sat down on a spider's web. The chimpanzee weighed next to nothing by now and lines of type could sometimes be seen running through it.

"The book must be checked out," said the head librarian sadly, "or . . . discarded."

The chimpanzee gave a pitiful howl. One hairy arm reached overhead with a grasping motion. Nicholas stared at that arm. Suddenly he understood.

"The birthday book!" he said, leaping up. The head librarian scrambled to her feet beside him.

"We looked there," said the librarian. "We looked everywhere."

"Maybe . . . just maybe . . ." said Nicholas. "It's worth a try. Think of cake and presents and – jump!"

They landed exactly on the page Nicholas remembered – the one with the cake and a great pile of presents.

"There," said Nicholas, pointing to a box with a green ribbon. A small blankness reached upward from the box lid. It was only for a blink of an eye, but Nicholas was sure of it now. That blank space could only be filled by the grasping arm of the lost chimpanzee. "There!"

The chimpanzee understood. With a whoop of delight, and a thrust of its arms that sent the ring spinning off Nicholas's finger, it hopped into the box.

The next moment they were sitting in the library.

"No wonder our friend couldn't find its way back," said the head librarian. "It had only seen the inside of the box."

"How did it get there? Who is the present for?" asked Nicholas.

"I was wondering that myself," said the head librarian.

So they read the book together, and for the first time in his life Nicholas did not even think once about building forts.

By the time they finished, it was evening. Everyone else had gone home . . . except Nicholas's mother. She'd fallen asleep with her head on a pile of books.

"I dreamed I was a bush pilot in the far north, a dancer in a grand ballet, and a detective on the trail of a master criminal!" she said.

The head librarian smiled at Nicholas. Sometimes a little magic in one part of the library spills over into other parts as well.

And Nicholas and his mother, their bag overflowing with books and their minds overflowing with wonder, walked home past the puddles of the warm spring night.